A TURKEY FOR THANKSGIVING

A TURKEY FOR THANKSGIVING

by Eve Bunting

Illustrated by Diane de Groat

Clarion Books

New York

Clarion Books
a Houghton Mifflin Company imprint
215 Park Avenue South, New York, NY 10003
Text copyright © 1991 by Eve Bunting
Illustrations copyright © 1991 by Diane de Groat

Watercolors were used to create the full-color artwork.
The typeface is 12 pt. Galliard.

For information about this and other Houghton Mifflin
trade and reference books and multimedia products,
visit The Bookstore at Houghton Mifflin on the
World Wide Web at (http://www.hmco.com/trade/).

Printed in the USA

Library of Congress Cataloging-in-Publication Data
Bunting, Eve, 1928–
A turkey for Thanksgiving / by Eve Bunting ;
illustrated by Diane de Groat.
     p.   cm.
Summary: Mr. and Mrs. Moose try to invite
a turkey to their Thanksgiving feast.
ISBN 0-89919-793-0   PA ISBN 0-395-74212-9
[1. Thanksgiving Day—Fiction.
2. Turkeys—Fiction. 3. Moose—Fiction.]
I. de Groat, Diane, ill. II. Title.
PZ7.B91527Tu 1991   [E]—dc20
90-21871   CIP   AC

WOZ 10 9 8

To Glenn, who insists on a turkey for Thanksgiving.
—E.B.

To Florence, and the memory of Thanksgivings past.
—D.D.

It was Thanksgiving morning. Mr. Moose helped
Mrs. Moose set the Thanksgiving table.

"Sheep will sit here. He likes a chair that's straight
up and down," Mr. Moose said. "Rabbit here.
Porcupine here. Mr. and Mrs. Goat here." He smiled
at his wife. "Isn't it nice to have friends to share
Thanksgiving?"

Mrs. Moose set two paper pilgrims, one at each end of the table. She placed the paper turkey with its great fan of a tail between the candles, and stood back.

"They look good, my dear," Mr. Moose said.

Mrs. Moose sighed. "Yes. But I wish we had a real turkey. Everyone always has a turkey for Thanksgiving. Everyone but us."

Mr. Moose nuzzled Mrs. Moose's head. "Well, that won't do. I will go this minute and find you a turkey for Thanksgiving."

Mr. Moose put on his cap and went out.

Mist wandered through the bare trees. The cold made his nose water.

Rabbit poked his head from his rabbit hole. "Mr. Moose! Is it dinnertime?"

"Not quite yet. Mrs. Moose wants a turkey. I'm off to find one."

Rabbit joined him in three quick hops. "I'll come, too."

Moose's warm breath hung white in front of him. Snow crunched under his hooves and made little holes that Rabbit jumped over.

"I see the Goats," Rabbit said.

Mr. Goat raised his head and spat out the tin can he was chewing. "Is it dinnertime?" he called.

"Not till I find a turkey," Mr. Moose said.

"We saw one down by the river," Mrs. Goat told him, and Mr. Goat added, "A fat one."

The Goats leaped down from their perch. "We'll show you."

Sheep was farther up the hillside, looking round as a fur ball in his winter coat. "Is it dinnertime?" he bellowed.

"First I have to find a turkey," Mr. Moose bellowed back.

"There's a turkey nest on the riverbank," Sheep called. "Wait for me."

The earth smelled of ice and moss as they crunched along. Above them a crow hung, black as a puff of wood smoke.

Porcupine was hiding in the underbrush.

"It's you," he said and put his quills down.

"We're off to get a turkey for Mrs. Moose," Mr. Moose explained. "Do you want to come?"

"I'm slow," Porcupine said. "Pick me up on your way back."

"Who'd want to pick you up?" Sheep asked, and laughed his bleat of a laugh.

"I'll wait," Porcupine told Mr. Moose.

They saw Turkey's nest right away, and Turkey himself peering over the top of it.

"Turkey! Turkey!" Mr. Moose called in his sweetest voice.

"Aagh!" Turkey blundered from his nest and ran.

Mr. Moose lumbered after him. "Turkey! Don't run. We just want you for Thanksgiving dinner."

Turkey ran faster.

Mr. Moose saw the red and blue sheen of Turkey's neck. Turkey's tail brushed crumbs of snow behind him as he tried to fly.

"Too fat," Mr. Goat said.

Turkey's legs bent in the middle as he fell.

Mr. Moose put a booted hoof on his head and smiled his great, toothy smile. "I hope you don't have other plans for Thanksgiving, Turkey."

He helped Turkey up. "My wife won't mind that you're too fat," he said. "Let's go. It's getting close to dinnertime."

They marched Turkey in front. "I'm sorry about this,
for I can see you don't want to come," Mr. Moose
said. "But I must insist. A promise is a promise."

There was a wreath of dried fruit on the Mooses'
door. Inside, the house was filled with Thanksgiving
smells. Mr. Moose hid Turkey behind him.

"Look who I brought, Mrs. Moose," he said.
"Sheep, the Goats, Rabbit, and Porcupine. And
ta-da!" He pushed Turkey around in front of
him. "For you. A turkey for Thanksgiving!"

Mrs. Moose clapped her hooves. "I'm *so* happy to have you, Turkey. Thank you, Mr. Moose. Now everything's perfect."

"Shall we sit?" Sheep asked, heading for the straight-up-and-down chair.

"Let's." Mrs. Moose pointed. "Rabbit here.

Porcupine here. Mr. and Mrs. Goat here, and look! I brought a chair from the other room in hopes of Turkey."

"A…a *chair*?" Turkey stammered.

"Right next to me," Mrs. Moose said. "Light the candles, Mr. Moose."

There were bowls of acorns and alfalfa sprouts, dried since summer. There was willow bark and cured grasses and wild parsley. There were pressed leaves, thin and pale as new ice on a pond.

"I hope you find something here to your liking, Mr. Turkey," Mrs. Moose said. "I wasn't sure of your taste."

"You are so kind to worry about my taste," Turkey said. "I thought you'd be worrying about *how* I'd taste."

"Heavens, no!" Mr. Moose smiled his big-toothed smile and filled everyone's cup with cold spring water. "It's so nice to have friends around the table at Thanksgiving."

Turkey's wattles wobbled. "It's even nicer to be AT your table and not ON it," he said. "Happy Thanksgiving, everybody."

"Happy Thanksgiving, Turkey."